GEORGE AND MARTHA
THE BEST OF FRIENDS

For My Mother

The stories in this book were originally published by
Houghton Mifflin Company in *George and Martha Round and Round.*
Copyright © 1988 by James Marshall
Copyright © renewed 2000 by Sheldon Fogelman

www.hmhco.com

First Green Light Readers edition, 2011

SANDPIPER and the SANDPIPER logo are trademarks of
Houghton Mifflin Harcourt Publishing Company.

Green Light Readers and its logo are trademarks of Houghton Mifflin Harcourt Publishing
Company, registered in the United States of America and/or other jurisdictions.

The Library of Congress has cataloged the hardcover edition as follows:
Marshall, James, 1942–1992.
George and Martha : round and round / written and illustrated by James Marshall.
p. cm.
Three of the stories that were originally published in
George and Martha : round and round, 1988.
Summary: Three stories chronicle the ups and downs of a
special friendship between two hippopotamuses.

ISBN: 978-0-618-98451-0 hardcover
ISBN: 978-0-547-51988-3 paperback

[1. Friendship–Fiction. 2. Hippopotamus–Fiction.] I. Title.
PZ7. M35672Gce 2008
[E]–dc22
2007025741

Manufactured in China
LEO 10 9 8 7 6 5 4 3 2
4500612326

GEORGE AND MARTHA
THE BEST OF FRIENDS

written and illustrated by
JAMES MARSHALL

sandpiper

Green Light Readers
HOUGHTON MIFFLIN HARCOURT
BOSTON   NEW YORK

TWO STORIES ABOUT THE BEST OF FRIENDS

STORY NUMBER ONE

THE ATTIC

One cold and stormy night
George decided to peek into the attic.
"Go on up," said Martha.
"Oooh no," said George.
"There might be a ghost up there,
or a skeleton, or a vampire,
or maybe even some werewolves."
"Oooh goody!" said Martha.
"Let's investigate."

But there wasn't much to see in the attic—
only a box of old rubber bands.

George was disappointed.

"Would you like to hear a story that will
give you goose bumps?" asked Martha.

"You bet," said George.

"When you hear it, your bones will go cold,"
said Martha.

"Oooh," said George.

"Your blood will curdle," said Martha.

"Ooooh," said George.

"And you'll feel mummy fingers up and
down your spine," said Martha.

"Stop!" cried George. "I can't take any more.
Tell me some other time!"

That night Martha went to bed
with the light on.
She had a bad case of goose bumps.

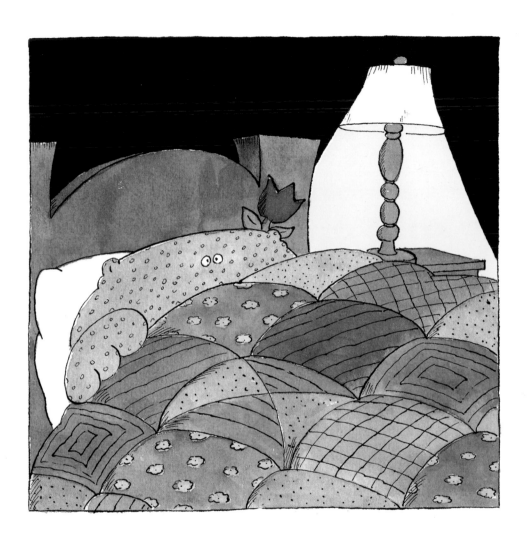

STORY NUMBER TWO

THE SURPRISE

One late-summer morning
George had a wicked idea.
"I shouldn't," he said.
"I really shouldn't."
 But he just couldn't help himself.
"Here comes the rain!" he cried.
"Egads!" screamed Martha.

Martha was thoroughly drenched
and as mad as a wet hen.
"That did it!" she said.
"We are no longer on speaking terms!"
"I was only horsing around,"
said George.
But Martha was unmoved.

The next morning, Martha read a funny story.

"I can't wait to tell George," she said.

Then she remembered that she and George

were no longer on speaking terms.

Around noon Martha heard a joke

on the radio.

"George will love this one," she said.

But she and George weren't speaking.

In the afternoon Martha observed

the first autumn leaf fall to the ground.

"Autumn is George's favorite season," she said.

Another leaf came swirling down.

"That does it," said Martha.

Martha went straight to George's house.

"I forgive you," she said.

George was delighted to be back
on speaking terms.

"Good friends just can't stay cross for
long," said George.

"You can say that again," said Martha.
And together they watched the
autumn arrive.

But when summer rolled around again,
Martha was ready and waiting.

JAMES MARSHALL (1942–1992)

is one of the most popular and celebrated artists in the field of children's literature. Three of his books were selected as New York Times Best Illustrated Books, and he received a Caldecott Honor award in 1989 for *Goldilocks and the Three Bears*. With more than seventy-five books to his credit, including the popular George and Martha series, Marshall has earned the admiration and love of countless readers.

Cryptogram

Unscramble the letters! Answers at the bottom of the page.

1. Where George peeked on a cold and stormy night.

    TICAT

2. George would feel these on his spine after he heard

    Martha's story. **R**EGIN**F**S

3. Martha left this on when she went to bed.

    HILGT

4. The kind of idea George had. **D**ECWIK

5. What George and Martha were not doing after he

    sprayed her. KASP**E**NIG

6. George's favorite season. MUTA**N**U

Magic Word: Unscramble the **BOLD** letters
to find the magic word!

Word Search

Find: skeleton, rubber, bones, summer, joke

S	U	M	M	E	R	A	C
N	K	B	H	C	I	M	B
E	V	E	O	G	W	F	O
M	D	G	L	Q	B	X	N
R	U	B	B	E	R	D	E
Y	L	S	Z	H	T	K	S
A	J	O	K	E	U	O	G
P	I	E	R	J	L	T	N

More fun activities to do at home!

• Draw a picture of the strange things you might find in your attic (or basement, garage, crawlspace, etc.).

• Do you know a story that will give your best friend goose bumps? Tell it! Or, write it down and draw some spooky pictures.

• Have you ever had a wicked idea you just couldn't resist? Write a story about what you did and what happened after you did it.

• Draw a picture of you and your best friend enjoying your favorite season.